The Last Prin
Saint-Domingue

A novel

by

Michelle St. Claire

Book 2 of Beautifully Unbroken™ Young Adult Series

The Last Princess of Saint-Domingue

ALSO BY MICHELLE ST. CLAIRE

Being Davanté

The Evolution of Max Fresh

A Garden for Raina

Cheap Justice

My Name is Marisol

A Tale of Two Brothers

Fighting Felicia

Carlos Solo

My Father's Soup

Fast Punk

Song of Sonya

The Last Princess of Saint-Domingue

ISBN: 9781945891038

Copyright 2016 Michelle St. Claire

Publisher: May3rdBooks, Inc.

Editor: MSB Editing Services

Cover Photo: Dora Alis

For Nya

A Prophecy

Dahomey, Africa
1783

Oh Nana, goddess of fertility, grant me a daughter, smooth and bright like the moon. Warm like the afternoon day. Smart like a tiger. Strong like the elephant's leg. Oh goddess of fertility, grant me a daughter-just one! One from my heart to be my sweetness, to sit with me and never go off to battle.

The Queen cried as she prayed with the most eloquent words of the Fongbe language. She was alone, prostrate on the ground, gently pressing her face to the dirt floor. At times her voice rose into a crescendo of loud wails, then returned to soft whimpering. Her body trembled. Her glowing brown skin dripped wet with sweat.

"Please," she said. "Please, please, please!"

The moon shone with indifference through the open

doorway. Its silver light casted a larger than life shadow of the Queen along the mud walls, yet she did not take notice. It was Mamma who had insisted she pray with swiftness. During her morning encounter with the old woman, the Queen revealed her heart's desire for a girl-child. Mamma patiently listened then warned the Queen that trouble was coming. As she talked, her worn face folded and flapped like a freshly washed batik skirt hung to dry. This trouble will be the final trouble, she foretold. It will end the kingdom. The finality in her tone sent shivers down the Queen's spine, prompting her to silently obey Mamma's urging.

As the Queen prayed, she suddenly imagined a beautiful newborn girl suckling at her breast. She vowed to the gods that she would protect this baby from King Fon, that the child would never be touched by him; that his violence would never trouble the promised girl.

A sudden soft breeze graced her wet skin. She lifted her head and slowly stood up, ignoring her stomach which growled with regret of missing the dinner meal. She smoothed her short curly hair, wiped her face, then walked towards the doorway.

"Queen!"

It was one of her maids. As the Queen stood beneath the moon's spotlight, she watched the little girl gradually emerge from the night.

"Queen!" the girl said as she bowed. "King Fon wants you."

"Tell him I am coming," said the Queen.

The girl nodded in obedience then scurried away. The Queen lingered outside, gazing at the night sky, wondering if this summons was an answer from the ancestors or a lure to her death. She sensed it was the latter. Her advanced age had caused her many nights with the king to cease long ago. King Fon considered any wife past twenty years old to be too old for childbirth. She had given him seven boys since her marriage, one for each year, beginning when she was 12 years old and he had killed them all.

Although the Queen never spoke of her distrust of King Fon, her bitterness soured her behavior towards him. Per chance, if he had arrived at her hut one day, she would not bow to him as required. During periods of his sickness, the Queen avoided reclining at his side to soothe him as was expected from his principal wife. And to bring the greatest offense to him, she had secretly re-named all her boys after the king offered them to the shaman for the blessing. She should have been sentenced to death long ago, but for some reason, King Fon never ordered it. Until this moment, the Queen was shamelessly confident of the king's pity for her. Until this moment, she had arrogantly believed he would never harm her.

The wind shifted. The Queen looked about her hut surmising she would see it no more. She splashed cool water from a nearby bucket onto her face and feet, delicately retied her skirt to the right side and slipped on leather sandals, fixing each one carefully. Then the Queen glided towards the king's chambers with a coolness she had never known. She followed the royal guards down the open air corridor leading to King Fon's quarters. The scent of meat cooking on a nearby fire tickled her nose. Despite the aroma, she was no longer hungry for she knew the ancestors would present a feast of her favorite foods once she passed through death. When they reached the king's chambers, the royal guards stopped and turned to her. The Queen closed her eyes and took a deep breath. Then, steadily, she placed her hand on the royal door and pushed.

The Last Annual Custom

Dahomey, Africa
1783

Mamma watched the smoke twirl and leap in the distance as if, it too, were dancing to the drums. Her spiritual ears heard tortured voices of captured prisoners rise from within the smoky clouds. This was the night of the Annual Custom, the night when the king's captors were mercilessly burned alive. Mamma envisioned hundreds of brown and black bodies twisting and jerking in a fiery pit, skin of men, women, and children slowly melting to ashes while their bones crackled and popped. They were souls in fright, screaming until they could scream no more.

Mamma closed her door. It would not be long until those tormented spirits visit her. Battle after battle, each one would slide under her door or glide through the windowless opening. Sometimes, a few timid souls would knock and wait for Mamma to open the door before entering. She never turned them away. In truth, they had done nothing wrong except live in a village that had lost a battle with King Fon.

The old woman's thoughts turned to the Queen whom she had not seen in days. She heard that the Queen had been summoned to King Fon's quarters one night but never returned, fueling rumors that the Queen's defiance had finally and fatally been checked. Mamma refused to believe it. The Queen was alive, this she knew. The gods had long ago told her that the Queen's survival was essential to the survival of the Fon people.

"Mamma?" said a child's soft voice.

"Yes?" said Mamma.

"Can I come in?"

"Come in."

A boy spirit melted through her mud door. His face appeared badly burned.

"I am scared. I don't want to die."

"Do not be afraid my child. Your journey to your

people's ancestors now begins."

"But I don't want to go. I want to go back home...to my mommy."

"Oh, child. Your mommy is waiting for you. She is waiting for you to join her with your people's ancestors."

"Will the journey be scary? Will I feel pain again?"

"You have endured all the pain you will ever feel. Your life on this land is finished. Now, you must join your people's ancestors."

The spirit boy looked about the room.

"Can I stay here?"

Mamma laughed.

"Oh, child. As much as I would love a companion, you cannot stay with me. You and I are of different people, different ancestors. You must remain with yours while I remain with mine."

"Are you sure I will see my mommy?"

"I am certain of this. You will see her very soon. In fact, she is now waiting for you."

The spirit boy left, melting through the door and disappearing in the night sky. Mamma sighed. She did not like to lie. If she had told him the truth, that he was killed as an offering to the King's ancestors, she feared he would never find rest. The boy spirit, like so many others before him, would commence to roaming the village in anger, in confusion or in wanderlust. Although most villagers were oblivious to such phenomena, it was only people like Mamma who suffered in silence from these foreign ghosts. So, for her own sanity and the safety of the Kingdom, Mamma had decided years ago to guide the spirits onward and away from the kingdom, urging them to return to their own ancestors.

"Pst!"

Mamma's attention was once again directed towards the door.

"Can I come in?"

"Yes."

A woman spirit melted through. Mamma spoke to her, politely encouraging her to go home. Throughout the night, Mamma received them in all forms, consoling them, empathizing with their pain. By daybreak, the heavy stench of death hung in the village air. The sheer number of spirits astounded Mamma. In all her years, she had never been as busy as she was last night. Mamma wondered if, this time, King Fon had gone too far.

A Vision

Dahomey, Africa
1783

The Queen embarked on a walk near the secret hut she had been living in. As she strolled, she heard whispers from within the soft rustle of the trees. Deep voices resonated with the rhythm of her own heartbeat. She stopped and closed her eyes. An image of a beautiful girl suddenly emerged in her mind.

A girl strong in frame, clothed in smooth brown skin was running in a forest. Her quick brown eyes were focused straight ahead. She wore a thin white dress and small leather sandals. In her right hand was a small stick. The girl waved the stick around as if fighting an invisible foe. Then she stopped and looked at the sky. Her light brown eyes were filled with moonlight.

The Queen suddenly felt a gentle thud in her womb.

The girl paused and whipped around toward a

sound only she could hear. Slowly, she backed away and ran back the way she came.

****

Mamma was ecstatic when she saw the Queen. Her belly was large and protruding.

"Oh, you are beautiful!" said Mamma.

The two women hugged quietly. Mamma held her close, feeling the baby shift in her mother's womb.

"Mamma," said the Queen. "I have so much to tell you."

Mamma motioned for the Queen to sit on the best chair in her hut.

"Sit, Queen, sit," she said.

The Queen raised her hand in protest.

"Oh, no Mamma. I can't sit. My back is too sore now."

Mamma ignored her, placing a bundle of clothes behind the Queen's back as she slowly sank into the chair.

"Tell me everything, daughter."

The Queen closed her eyes momentarily and shook her head.

"Mamma, so much has happened. I thought I was going to die," said the Queen. "I thought the king was going to send me back to the ancestors."

"What happened?"

"The king was so angry. His eyes were red. He was ugly with hate for me. He yelled. He screamed. He ordered the guards to take me! Then, I cried. I cried for all my children, all my sons he killed. The king's face changed like the shifting wind. He said he was sorry and he told me to come to him."

"Did you?"

"I thought he was trying to trick me. But I realized I had no choice. If my end was near, it was near. So, I went to him. He held me and soothed my head. He told me not to worry."

"The king? King Fon? I can't believe what I am hearing! The king? *Soothing you?*"

"Yes! He tried to make me feel better. He told the guards to leave and he led me to a special hut outside the kingdom. It is a secret place. He took me there and laid with me as if he loved me."

Mamma pondered her words. The king had twenty-four wives. He governed a vast kingdom. He was prudent with provisions. He was ruthless in war. Only at special times, was he respectful to his wives, but never was the king loving, Mamma thought. It was a gesture the king did not know.

"Mamma, I had never felt this in my life. Afterwards, he ordered the cook to make me whatever I wanted. He left the next morning and ordered the guards to protect me. For days, the cook brought me wonderful food and I lived alone in peace."

"Then what happened?"

"The king never came back. When I started to feel the sickness, I sent a guard to summon the king but he did not come. Instead, he returned a message that I was granted to stay in the secret hut for as long as I needed. The king promised to give me my freedom quietly after the baby was born. He even promised to give me half his kingdom and send me away secretly lest I am hunted by his enemies."

"This cannot be. The king has never done this. Who has heard of such things?"

"Mamma, I have been afraid to trust his words, too. But look at me! Seven new moons have passed and my child is growing happily within me. I am well fed and well protected. It is true."

Mamma leaned back, swallowing the heaviness in the air. She had not seen this. Mamma had not been given the sight to predict this. It could only mean one thing. The ancestors were about to do something greater than Mamma could comprehend.

"Queen, this is good news."

The Queen shook her head in agreement, her eyes moist with happy tears.

"There is more, Mamma. I believe I have just seen my baby in a vision. It is a girl."

Mamma sat up.

"Tell me everything, Queen. Tell me what you saw."

For the next hour, Mamma quietly listened to the

Queen's words as she recanted her vision of the girl-child.

"The ancestors are speaking," said Mamma. "This child will be born between death and life, between past and future."

"I don't understand. Whose life? Whose death?"

"The kingdom's death. New life on new lands. And-."

"What is it, Mamma?"

"That's all. I am tired. I have to lay down. Old woman tired."

The End of the Kingdom

Dahomey, Africa
1783

Mamma awakened to the smell of fear. She clamored out of her bed and shuffled towards the door. Through a small crack, Mamma saw the twinkling of a hundred stars in the night sky, illuminating a deserted village. Not one person was milling about.

Mamma scratched her head.

"Where are the night guards?" she said to herself.

It was a crime punishable by death for any of the royal guards to abandon his post. Many times Mamma had mournfully watched a guilty guard plunge his own sword into his chest. The guards deemed it was better to die at their own hands then to fall under the king's wrath.

Quickly, Mamma dressed. She hastily slipped her feet into her worn leather sandals. She grabbed a cloth bag and mindlessly packed all the food she had stored in her hut, throwing in medicine bottles, tea leaves, and homemade ointments. She wrapped her head with an old headscarf of blue, orange, and white. She flung the bag over her shoulder. Then Mamma fled.

She ran. Her skinny aged legs miraculously regained its youth, hurdling through the forest, ignoring the pokes from thistles and wayward branches. Mamma leaped over ditches. She quickened her pace, realizing the stars' especially bright luminance was intentional. As the Queen's secret hut emerged in the distance, Mamma took a deep breath before sprinting across the open field. When she reached the door, she did not wait to knock. She thrust it open with all her strength.

"Queen!" said Mamma.

The Queen was lying on her bed in half slumber. She laid on her left side so as to accommodate her swollen stomach.

"Queen!" said Mamma, louder.

The Queen sat up slowly.

"Mamma, what is it? Even the birds are still sleeping! What is so important at this hour?"

"Rise. Dress. Gather your belongings. We must go

now. I will explain it on the way. Trouble is upon the kingdom. King Fon's hour is soon arriving."

"What do you mean?"

Mamma did not reply. She scurried around the Queen and supported her as she rose from the bed. Then Mamma began packing a bag with the Queen's clothes.

"Mamma! Speak. You are frightening me!"

"My child, long ago, King Fon was not a king. He was merely a man, but he was lost. He was a wanderer of the earth. He made many bad turns, earning the wrath of the gods but they spared him. They delayed his punishment…until now."

"Oh, Mamma. I do not understand your words. What punishment? What did the King do?"

"No time. We have no time. Here, put this on."

The Queen sighed, slipping on the dress Mamma gave her. The two fled without making a sound, running west towards the sea.

"Mamma! Queen! Wait!"

Mamma and the Queen slowed to see several kingdom women behind them.

"Let us follow you," said the women.

The Queen recognized one of them as a maid to King Fon. She remembered the maid had recently had a baby.

"Where is your child, woman?" asked the Queen to the maid.

"I am Enibokun…Eni. Oh, my Queen, my child is with the ancestors! She was killed by the White men!" she said.

"White men?" asked the Queen.

"Yes. King Fon and his army had been fighting the White men. My child was playing outside and I thought at least one guard would be watching my child but there was no one! I found my child lying lifeless on the dusty earth with the White man's rock in his heart. My child! My child!"

Eni collapsed to the ground in grief and sorrow, prompting her companion to console her.

"Women! Not now. If we do not hurry, we will have more reasons to cry," said Mamma.

She was angered by the stop. The ancestors were

commanding her to keep moving, to keep running towards the sea.

"Let's go!" she said.

They ran in single file so as to support each other should one of them fall or lag behind. Mamma made sure to keep the Queen behind her since it was the Queen's life Mamma knew the gods sought to spare. The women ran steadily in the late twilight. Day eventually broke with the sun's first rays peeking through the African clouds. When the women grew tired, they stopped to take shelter under a large dika tree. Mamma leaned her back against it, exhaling loudly. Never had she run so far so fast.

"Mamma, please," said the Queen breathlessly. "Tell me, what is happening?"

Mamma was resting with her eyes closed, waiting for the ancestors' direction.

"Mamma!" said the Queen again.

Mamma opened her eyes and turned to her.

"I'm sorry, my child. I did not hear you."

"Mamma, I want to know the truth. No more waiting. I want to know right now!"

The other women shifted their attention towards Mamma in anticipation.

"Queen, there is too much to say. I do not have the time right now. Soon, we must continue."

"Continue to where? Where are we going?"

"To the sea. It is the only way. You must leave the kingdom."

"Why?"

Suddenly, a loud bang vibrated through the trees. Shouts and wailing could be heard throughout the land. Birds cried frantically as they escaped their nestled homes, flapping their wings wild in terror.

"Come!" Mamma said.

She motioned for the women to follow her once again.

This time they moved slowly and cautiously. The Queen's baby nervously shifted in her womb triggering beads of sweat to grace her face. She stopped to wipe her brow.

"No, Queen. You must keep going," said Mamma.

The Queen tried to keep up, but could not. She

trailed behind the small group. The weight of her womb were like sacks of stones to her lower back. Eventually, the Queen lagged so far behind she could no longer see Mamma.

The loud bang repeated, reverberating all around them. It seemed they were in the middle of a fierce battle. Screams of women and children grew near.

Bang! Bang! Bang!

As the women moved, the chaotic sounds grew louder. Again, the Queen stopped and leaned against a tree to wipe her face. Looking up from where she stood, she saw a beautiful bird perched on a branch, staring at her curiously. She remembered when she played among such trees as a child, how she used to flap her wings, imitating the birds, studying their beauty and freedom. She suddenly felt an overwhelming desire to soar, too, to spread her wings and fly away.

"Queen!"

Mamma ran towards her. Her legs leapt over the rocks and branches like a deer.

"Queen!" said Mamma as she approached.

The Queen wanted to move forward, but she could not. A sudden pain struck her lower stomach, forcing her to cry out in agony.

"Ah!" said the Queen.

A small river of blood emerged, running down the Queen's leg, pooling around her feet.

"Oh, no. This is too soon!" said Mamma.

The ancestors had told Mamma that the child would be born on the ship, not here on kingdom land. She cursed herself for ordering the Queen to run so fast in her condition.

Mamma guided the Queen to the ground.

"Here, Queen. Sit down," she said.

Then Mamma called for Eni who had been running ahead, turned around and obediently ran back while the rest of the group continued.

"Eni," she said. "Go into my bag and pull out some clothes, a knife and my medicine bottles."

Eni obeyed, returning with the items in seconds.

"Now, hold the Queen's legs."

"What?"

"Hold her legs!"

Eni braced the Queen's legs.

"Queen, take a deep breath and push!" said Mamma.

The Queen closed her eyes, imagining her daughter in her arms, marveling at her baby's beautiful bright skin reflecting the sun's glory.

"Good! Push again."

The Queen focused on her stomach and pushed with all her might, pretending not to see the look of panic on Eni's face. This child was her baby girl, the girl she had repeatedly asked the ancestors for. This was her princess, her beautiful princess.

"Good! Good! Almost!"

The Queen cried as she pushed again.

"There she is!"

The baby wailed loudly. Mamma held her up and expertly sliced the umbilical cord. Then she stood up and quickly offered the baby to the ancestors and gods for their blessing. After cleansing the baby with the liquid from her medicine bottles, she gave the baby girl to the Queen.

"Princess," said the Queen to her daughter.

Mamma knelt down next to the Queen.

"Queen, I must tell you the truth. I should not have pushed you so hard," she said.

"Oh, no. It was not your fault. This child came when she was ready to come. Now I finally have my girl!" said the Queen, caressing her daughter's face.

"Queen, you will not go with her. You will remain here. The girl-child will continue on...without you."

Tears welled in the Queen's eyes.

"What do you mean, Mamma?"

"It is the wisdom from the ancestors and the decision of the gods."

The Queen held her baby close, burying her nose in her soft hair. Then she opened her dress and exposed her breast to her infant for feeding.

"Mamma, look!" said Eni in a whisper.

Following Eni's gaze, Mamma saw White men armed with swords. They were moving closer to the women although Mamma could tell the White men had not yet seen them.

Mamma turned to the Queen.

"Give the baby to Eni," she said.

The Queen ignored Mamma, clutching the infant closer to her breast.

"Queen, you must. Eni will take her to the sea. There, they will embark on new lands. If you keep her, she will die."

The Queen cried unashamedly for she refused to let her child go. In desperation, Mamma slipped her arms around the infant and gently pulled her from the Queen's grasp. The two women struggled for a few minutes before the Queen finally released. Mamma took off her colorful headscarf and wrapped the newborn in it. Then she placed the baby in Eni's arms and ordered her to run to the sea.

"Eni, you will be taken," said Mamma. "You will be brought low and humbled, but the baby will not be harmed. Take her and raise her as your own. Remember she is royalty. She is the daughter of a Queen. Do *not* let her go!"

Eni listened intently to Mamma's words, nodding in obedience. Then she took the Queen's hand, kissed it and bowed in the customary manner. Taking a deep breath,

Eni hugged the newborn close to her chest and darted away. The Queen wailed. She tried to stand up to run after Eni, but her legs buckled beneath her.

Despite the early morning hour, the air was thick with grief and sadness. The White men were hundreds of feet away from them now. Mamma could hear the rustling of nearby trees and bushes as the men made their way closer.

"Queen, whatever you do, do not resist. They may spare you."

Before the Queen could question Mamma's words, a White man finally spotted them, calling out excitedly in French.

"Here, Captain Marcelon!"

In seconds, the two women were surrounded by White men with their guns and swords drawn. A tall, heavy-set man emerged, walking closer to Mamma and the Queen. The Queen grabbed Mamma's hand and squeezed it.

"What do you want?" said Mamma.

Captain Marcelon did not understand Fongbe. He

wrinkled his brow in confusion.

"I said, what do you want? Take me! Spare the Queen," said Mamma, gesturing to the Queen.

Captain Marcelon looked at the Queen, noticing dried blood caked on the grass around her.

"Get up!" he said in French.

The Queen did not move. She clung to Mamma.

"Get up!" he said again.

Mamma looked at the Queen and nodded, indicating that she should go with them. So the Queen slowly stood up, leaning against the tree for support. Her clothes were soaked with blood from child birth.

"Look, she is sick," said Captain Marcelon. "She will not fetch a good price. Get rid of her...and the old woman."

"Sir, maybe she is not that sick," said a short White man. "She looks young. Perhaps she can breed, no?"

Captain Marcelon moved closer to the Queen to study her. He was a tall, ugly man, rough and slovenly in appearance. His hair, oily and unwashed, framed an unshaven face stained with soot and dried sweat. He moved even closer to the Queen. With the tip of his sword, he attempted to lift up her dress but the Queen refused his disrespectful gesture. She slapped him.

Mamma shrieked.

"Queen, no!" she said.

It was too late. A Frenchman armed with a musket gun quickly loaded it and pointed it at the Queen. It made a loud smoky bang, then she fell backwards. Mamma cried out. She gathered the lifeless Queen in her arms. But as quickly as the man could reload, Mamma suffered the same fatal demise. She fell with a huff, exhaling slowly as her spirit detached from her body. Mamma spirit then took hold of Queen spirit, commencing their journey to their ancestors. Along the way, Mamma spirit reassured Queen spirit that the girl-child would be spared, that she would live a long life in freedom.

Middle Passage

Atlantic Ocean
1783

Eni was naked. Her neck and ankles were encased in heavy iron shackles. She laid on her back chained to a plank bed, struggling to breathe in hot dense air. Every now and then, warm urine flowed around her. The putrid stench of human feces stung Eni's eyes and nostrils.

She kept track of the days by watching the moonlight flickering through slits in the ship's hull. They had been on a ship for two new moons and despite their horrid state, the Queen's baby was still alive. Eni could feel the soft rise and fall of the infant next to her. Still wrapped in Mamma's colorful headscarf, the baby was tightly wedged within Eni's underarm, blissfully slumbering.

She was amazed at the infant's resiliency. Weeks ago along the African shore, Eni had been beaten, stripped, and shackled by her neck and feet alongside her kinswomen. When they had boarded the large ship, Eni saw several of King Fon's royal guards thrown overboard. Their pride prevented them from accepting such humility at the hands of White men. Some royal guards viciously fought the White men, earning them instant execution by drowning for such insolence. At first, Eni wanted to join them, desiring to jump in the enticing blue waters and break free of the impending misery that awaited her, but she could not shake Mamma's admonition to her. For the sake of the Queen's baby, Eni decided to find the will to survive.

Yet the hope of survival decreased with every passing night. Each morning, several of her kinsmen and kinswomen did not awaken. Their bodies, stiff with rigor, quietly rotted among them. Only when their mortal stench reached the upper deck, did White men come down, holding their noses, coughing, and wiping their eyes. Some of the Africans speculated that the bodies were burned while others said they were thrown into the sea. Eni hoped the waters claimed them so as to have an easier journey to the afterlife.

As she laid, Eni painfully turned her head to gaze at the infant. The baby had miraculously grown fat. Her plump cheeks glistened in the shadows, oblivious to the Africans' humiliating plight. When awake, the infant often sang her gibberish songs amidst groans of those around her, naïve to the reality of what was happening; that an entire African kingdom had been sold into slavery. Some Africans prayed for death. Others called the gods to save them. Clinging to Mamma's words about survival, Eni tried to find stillness in her heart. While others prayed for death, she often closed her eyes in the cramped space and prayed for life.

Occasionally, White men would bring her and other mothers and their children to the upper deck. Eni, chained by the neck to the women before and behind her, would clutch the Queen's baby under her arm as they were dragged upstairs. For several precious minutes, Eni would breathe in the clean ocean air. At those times, she tried to eavesdrop on the White men's conversations. Although she did not understand French, Eni had been able to make out two words: "Saint-Domingue." Noticing that the

White men said those words repeatedly in their speech, she concluded that Saint-Domingue was the ship's final destination. Each time when Eni and the other mothers returned to the hull, the Africans called out in agony to the White men. They pled for food, for water, for medicine, but the White men ignored them. They simply re-chained the mothers to their planks before quickly returning to the upper deck.

In the midst of the Africans' misery, arguments often broke out amongst those who still had strength to speak. Most of the conversations were among the survivors of King Fon's royal army. Some African soldiers hotly expressed their anger for the defeat of the king.

"He was ambushed!" said one soldier.

"Yes, he was caught from behind and killed," said another.

"It was our enemy who did it," said another anonymous voice.

"Where is the King's principal son, Omorédé, eh?" asked an angry soldier.

A hush fell over them as they waited for a voice to acknowledge the king's lineage. A few minutes later, a weak voice whispered.

"Here. I am here," said the voice.

Eni was astonished that the king's principal son was captured. He was young and should have been able to outrun the Frenchmen. She could not believe her ears. Tears suddenly ran down the sides of her face. If the king's son could not escape such tragedy, then how will I survive? Will the Queen's baby even live through this journey? she thought to herself.

"Why are you here?" asked the angry soldier. "You should have died with your father!"

His tone was intentionally disrespectful. In kingdom land, he would have been reprimanded swiftly for proposing such a question to royalty, but here, lying in filth in the belly of a ship, such customs no longer seemed necessary.

"I-I fought valiantly but I was overtaken by the White man," said Omorédé.

"Look at us!" said the angry soldier. "Look at us!

We are treated worse than dogs. We are dying in chains!"

"Quiet, Mudia!" said an anonymous voice.

"No," said Mudia. "I will not be quiet anymore. If this is my last breath, I will speak my mind!"

"Mudia, watch your tongue," said another anonymous voice.

"Omorédé, where is your royalty now, eh?" said Mudia. "When did you fight for your people? When?"

"You do not know everything. My father, King Fon, was struck from behind. He instantly fell to his death. I did not know this until nightfall. That is when our enemy invaded the kingdom and sold us to the White man," said Omorédé.

"This is not true! You are lying. I saw you running away with the King," said Mudia.

"I tell you, if I ran away, I would not be here. I am here because I stayed and I fought," said Omorédé.

"Eh! Liar! I lost my wife and my children because of you. You are not royalty; you are a coward!" said Mudia.

Several people gasped at his brashness.

"I-I am the only royalty here. You must still respect me," said Omorédé.

Although Eni did not want to interfere in the conversation, she feared for the life of the Queen's baby. She hoped that if all knew this infant was royalty, too, they would protect her should Eni not survive. So Eni cleared her parched throat before speaking. Her lips painfully cracked and bled as she opened her mouth.

"No," said Eni as loudly as she could. "He is not the only royalty. Here is the principal Queen's baby at my breast."

"What? The Queen? She is *dead*?" asked a voice in disbelief.

"I fear so. I left Mamma and the Queen on the edge of kingdom land. They did not follow me," said Eni.

A woman's voice interjected.

"If this is the Queen's baby, then she is royalty. We must treat her as so," she said.

"Yes," said another voice. "The baby is the last of the king's line. She is the last royal child."

"No, the king's son is greater than her," said a man.

"This cannot be. Omorédé is a coward! I saw him run away, too. He left the kingdom exposed!" said another soldier.

At this, they argued amongst themselves about who should succeed in King Fon's place.

"I know," said an older man. "This is how it will be. Omorédé will no longer claim the throne. It will be the Queen's baby. She is Nyashia, princess. We will call her Nya."

"Yes, this is just. This will be the correct way," said a woman.

"She cannot lead anyone. I am king now! *I* am the king's principal son!" said Omorédé.

"Eh! I saw you, you coward," said Mudia. "You deserted the people. You do not deserve to be king!"

"People," said a man. "Why are we fighting? Look at us, we are bound like animals on the way to our death. What does it matter? We have no leader now but the White man."

"Never! The White man will never be my leader!" said Mudia.

Others joined in with shouts of agreement.

"But, my people," said a woman. "If we survive this journey, we will need a symbol; someone who will keep us united or else our ways will be forgotten."

"Yes, this is a good idea," said Mudia.

"Woman!" said an anonymous voice to Eni. "Can you lift up Nya?"

Eni painfully lifted her arm from where Nya was cradled. She held her up in the air as far as the chains would allow. Nya whimpered softly in bewilderment. Her little hand clutched a corner of Mamma's bright colorful scarf.

"Gods of our ancestors," said the woman. "Raise up this child to lead us into freedom. Bless her and keep her healthy and strong. Give her benefits and all the best this miserable life will afford. May she be instrumental in our fight for freedom and justice!"

The Africans jeered in a brief moment of celebration. Women on either side of Eni reached to touch Nya in customary gestures of respect.

Interception

Atlantic Ocean
1783

Captain Marcelon wrung his hands. He was only days away from Saint-Domingue, traveling at a good pace until the flags of the French Navy were spotted early that morning. It took only hours for the massive French ship of the line to speed towards his ship. The Navy was now only knots away now.

"Lock the doors! Clean up that blood!" Captain Marcelon said to his deck hands.

"Sir, what do we do with the cargo?" asked one of them.

"Do not worry about them, Wilhelm. I will take care of it."

"Yes, sir."

Captain Marcelon knew this journey was a risk. The French Navy were purportedly enforcing Code Noir, although no one obeyed it. All French merchants knew the

Code's threat of heavy fines was just a pretext for the king's men to augment their salaries with bribes.

"Captain Marcelon," said Thierry, his best deck hand.

"What is it?" said Captain Marcelon.

"We are low on ammunition."

"How can this be? We had plenty before we came to Africa."

"Yes, but our stock pile was stolen by King Fon's men in battle. We never found them."

Captain Marcelon exhaled loudly. He was tired of trading in human cargo. The Africans were more trouble than they were worth in his estimation. Although they seemed like savages to most French, Captain Marcelon found them to be cleverer than most people realized.

"Gather what we have and assume your positions," said Captain Marcelon. "And Thierry, throw all the babies overboard. I do not want their annoying little voices to be heard!"

Thierry nodded in obedience. He turned around and immediately repeated the command to Wilhelm who gulped loudly.

"We have to kill their *babies*?" said Wilhelm.

Thierry grabbed a leather whip hanging on a nearby wooden post and wound it around his arm.

"Wilhelm, are you disobeying Captain Marcelon's orders?" said Thierry.

Wilhelm backed away.

"No-no," he said.

He scurried to the flat door leading to the hull, then swung it open and bound down the steps. Immediately greeted by the stench, Wilhelm held his nose while descending further. Some Africans called out to him in their native tongues while others yelled at him in anger. Willem scanned the hull for babies, feeling certain there were none in this lot. He remembered the last trade; it was the worst journey of his life. They had captured an African village full of small children. Several times, Willem attempted to kill himself by jumping overboard after having witnessed the death of most of those children.

Relieved of not finding a baby, Wilhelm turned around and rushed back to the door. Just as he reached for it, he heard a whimper. Hiding beneath a woman's arm, he saw a small infant, surprisingly plump with smooth brown skin. The woman, obviously emaciated, caught his eye and stared.

"Wilhelm! Did you find anything?" said Thierry from the upper deck.

Wilhelm did not answer. The infant stared at him with brown eyes so big, he sensed she could see into his soul or rather the spittle on his hands from choking sick slave children to death and throwing them overboard to drown. He wondered if the infant could see the old marks on his arms where young slave girls bit and clawed when he dragged them to Captain Marcelon's bedroom.

"Wilhelm! Did you find anything?" said Thierry again.

Wilhelm responded with a meek, "No."

"What?" said Thierry.

The infant suddenly smiled at him.

"No," he said, louder. "There is nothing here."

"All hands on deck...*now*!" said Thierry.

The sun was now at its highest point in the sky,

unforgiving in its forceful heat. After much preparation, Captain Marcelon ordered his deck hands to take their positions. The ship's two cannons were now aimed at the nearing French Navy. All hands stood down, awaiting the Captain's signal.

The French Royal Navy ship of the line was one of the biggest Captain Marcelon had ever seen. There were two-decks of 90 to 130 powder guns, 1,000 soldiers in immaculate blue waistcoats with gold buttons glinting in the hot sun. The soldiers worked in orderly fashion as they quickly lowered their plank onto Captain Marcelon's ship for the French General to come aboard.

General Damien Leandré Bufort was tall and menacing. He stepped onto Captain Marcelon's ship calmly, with his hands clasped behind his back. After strolling around for a few minutes, he greeted the Captain with a smirk.

"So, this is what you do? You are a pitiful *merchant*?" said General Bufort.

Captain Marcelon shrugged his shoulders.

"I am just a merchant trying to make a living," he

said.

"Hm. You have heard of Code Noir, no? It was yet another of King Louis' attempt to curry favor with his annoying political hypocrites! I am certain you have heard of it…and I am certain you are in violation."

"I would never disobey the French Crown."

"Hm, we shall see. Where are the slaves, eh?"

"Oh no, General. We have no human cargo here, only beans and tea leaves.

"Is this right? Beans and tea leaves? Your hull requires ventilation holes for beans and tea leaves?"

"We have a very unique business."

General Bufort scoffed. He looked around again, noticing a freshly washed floor.

"Captain Marcelon, are you aware of the penalties of violating Code Noir? It not only applies to landowners, but to anyone who owns slaves no matter how transitory the ownership?"

The General gazed at the deck hands. They were a pitiful group of Frenchmen, dirty and poorly dressed. One of them had a leather belt wrapped around his waist. The

General knew such tools were not used for fashion, but rather to keep human cargo in line. General Bufort swung around to face Captain Marcelon, looking directly into his eyes.

"Captain Marcelon, do not lie to me. I am on order from the French Crown. Do not prevent me from executing my duties."

Before Captain Marcelon could respond, an infant cry suddenly bellowed from below the deck. Captain Marcelon's face flushed. He gave a sideways glance to Thierry, who promptly looked away.

"What was that? *A baby*? You keep a *baby* in the hull? Even savage babies are treated better! That is torture! This is not a good situation for you, Captain."

Captain Marcelon did not know how to respond. As the baby's cries grew louder, General Bufort followed the sound, which led him to a non-descript door bolted along the deck floor.

"Unlock it" said General Bufort.

The Captain's stomach turned. He held up his hands in protest.

"General, please."

"Again, you are preventing me from executing the King's orders?"

"No. I am asking you to not open that door. I have my wife and child there. My wife is very, very sick."

General Bufort pulled a pipe from his front pocket. He snapped his fingers and one of his soldiers ran over to light it. After a few puffs, he leaned closer to the Captain.

"Hm. It seems you have a situation and I have a job to do. Maybe the value of your situation is worth more to you than my job."

Captain Marcelon knew he was now in a trap. If the bribe was not large enough, it could backfire, leading him to be hanged for such impropriety.

"General, all merchants value their goods highly."

General Bufort coughed roughly, clearing out smoke from his throat.

"Captain, how valuable are your beans and tea leaves?"

"To me, General, to my customers who are waiting for them, they are worth thirty-thousand francs."

"Thirty-thousand francs? That is the value of your cargo? Hm. That is very good. You are a very good merchant."

Soft raindrops suddenly began pelting their backs. The afternoon sky had swiftly darkened, threatening an impending storm. General Bufort was apparently not pleased with the sudden change in weather. He angrily put out his pipe.

"Captain Marcelon, the King pays me five thousand francs per cargo to investigate. Five thousand. That is *my* value."

The Captain motioned to Thierry to come near, then quickly whispered something into his ear. Thierry nodded and hurried away. Seconds later, he returned with Captain Marcelon's money bag.

"General Bufort, if you were in my employ, I could do better than the King."

"Oh? How much better?"

"Ten thousand francs."

A rumble of thunder vibrated through the sky. Lightning flashed. General Bufort grabbed the bag from the Captain's hands and threw it to one of his soldiers. He waited for his soldier to open it, look inside, then signal with an approving nod.

"Captain Marcelon, you are a good merchant. My job is now done. I do not find a violation of Code Noir because I do not see any slaves. Keep your cargo safe as you journey through these unforgiving seas."

General Bufort backed away from the door and hastened across the plank onto his own ship. Once off board, the General turned, tipped his hat to Captain Marcelon, then disappeared into his quarters. At that moment, the skies suddenly unleashed peels of thunder and rumbling. Only after the French Navy ship gradually pull away and turn in a northern direction did the Captain finally exhale.

Landfall

Tortuga Island, Saint-Domingue
1783

Eni shivered. Every fiber of her being increased in temperature the longer she stood beneath the tropical sun. Despite her condition, she clutched Nya closely.

"Stand up!" said Captain Marcelon to an African.

They had de-boarded upon reaching land. Eni and the other Africans were conjoined in long iron chains around their neck and feet as they stood before a small crowd.

"Thierry, get the key, that one is dead," said Captain Marcelon.

Thierry obeyed, returning with a large iron key. He squeezed himself between the rows of men that stood in front of Eni's row of women. The African men were unable to stand on account of a stiff, dead body. Thierry unchained his neck brace and pushed the deceased out of the way, then snapped his fingers, signaling for someone to pick up the body.

"Dump it in the sea," said Thierry.

Some of the African men groaned in protest. Eni closed her eyes and prayed. She could not bear to see their kinsman disposed of so cruelly.

"Quiet!" said a deck hand, lashing his whip.

"Sir, they are ready," said Thierry to Captain Marcelon.

The Captain nodded. He went to the port entrance and whispered to some people. Soon, a heavy set White man emerged from the crowd, fully dressed, walking with a wooden cane.

"Shall I inspect? After all, Blaise, we are both businessmen," he said.

"Of course, Claude, they are all good," said Captain Marcelon.

Claude Douleur huffed in reply. He walked closer to the row of Africans, beginning with the men. At each man, he inspected their eyes, their mouths and their muscles. Some of the men protested Claude's protrusion, especially Mudia. Eni could hear him refusing to submit to Claude's handling. Mudia flinched wildly while mumbling curses beneath his breath. Claude swiftly smacked Mudia on his back with his cane, causing the African to double over in pain.

"This slave is a defiant one," said Claude.

Like many of the Africans, Mudia had learned a few French words, including the word for slave.

"Slave, no," said Mudia.

Claude raised his eyebrows.

"You speak French, eh?" he said.

"Slave, no. Never slave!" said Mudia.

Claude took off his hat and handed it to a servant standing nearby. He coolly raised his cane above his head and beat Mudia repeatedly until he was spitting blood.

"You are a slave. You are *my* slave. I own you. You will do what I say."

"Slave, no."

Claude commenced to beating him again. Mudia buckled over as he received the unmerciful blows until Claude eventually grew tired. The overweight man was sweating profusely under the hot tropical sun.

"Blaise, you have given me much more work to do. I will not pay full price for this one."

Claude waited as Mudia managed to stand up again. Mudia's face was bloodied and rapidly swelling, his back was covered with open wounds that exposed his flesh. He squinted at Claude through swelling eyes and hot anger.

"Slave. No."

Claude was taken aback by Mudia's defiance. Such a painful and humiliating beating should have broken him, but it did not.

Claude turned to Captain Marcelon.

"These slaves are different."

Captain Marcelon shrugged his shoulders.

"They are all the same to me. You made an order and we delivered."

Claude took a long look at Mudia before moving on to the next man. He continued his inspection of the entire line of African men.

"Fine, the men are fine."

Captain Marcelon snapped his fingers to Thierry.

"Get them ready for sail to Port-au-Prince," he said.

"Yes, sir," said Thierry.

The rows of African men were led back onto the sandy shore. Mudia walked gingerly on account of his painful wounds. He was ordered to sit down on the hot sand on Tortuga beach to wait for Claude to finish the sale.

"Now, the women. You know that I am *very* particular about them," said Claude.

Claude repeated his inspection of each African woman as he had done with the men. Yet he found the women to have more issues.

"This one looks sick."

"This one is too old."

"Not this one."

"Take her out."

Captain Marcelon tried to salvage them to no avail. Reluctantly, he ordered Thierry to remove the ones Claude rejected. Claude continued his merciless inspection until he stopped in front of Eni.

"A baby wrapped in fancy clothes. Interesting. Is it alive?"

The Captain snapped his fingers for a deck hand, but Thierry did not appear as he was preoccupied with preparing the men for sail to Port-au-Prince. When he saw Wilhelm standing idly by, the Captain gestured for him to inspect the baby. Wilhelm reluctantly agreed. He went to Eni and proceeded to take the baby away from her but Eni cried loudly and closed her entire body over Nya. The commotion shook Nya out of her slumber, causing her to scream.

"Ah! That is enough. No need to take the baby. I just wanted to know if it was alive," said Claude.

Eni cradled Nya to soothe her cries.

"Well," said Claude. "The mother *is* strong. I suppose she just needs to eat, Blaise. She has been nursing, that is why she looks so small, no?"

Claude eyed Eni again. She was sweating profusely now. Her face winced in annoyance at his protruding stare.

"What is the baby?" asked Claude. "If it is a boy, I do not want the mother. If it is a girl, then I will take the mother, but at half price. In time, the girl will compensate for her sick mother."

Wilhelm stepped closer to Eni and reached for Nya. His hands trembled. Sweat coursed down his face. Carefully, he took Nya out of Eni's arms and unwrapped her from the scarf. He held her up for Claude to see.

"Ah, good. Fine. I will take both," said Claude.

Then he turned to the next slave woman in the line until he finished his inspections. Out of the sixty-three women, he chose only fourteen, crushing Captain Marcelon's profits.

"Claude, sir, you asked for at least one hundred," said Captain Marcelon.

"Yes, Blaise, but you gave me useless ones with no value. That is not what we bargained for."

"There is nothing wrong with them! They are all fertile."

"How do you know? I purchased some last month and only two out of the fifty have bred."

"Yes, but you did not purchase them from *me*. When have I failed you, my friend?"

"Touché. You have persuaded me. Fine, I will take

twenty more."

The ship sailed quickly for the wind was behind its sails. Salty tropical air graced Eni's nose with the smell of thick forests, wet mountain rock, and abundant fish swimming beneath them. Eni suddenly recalled Mamma's words. As she saw the green island with large mountains appear in the distance, she realized this was the new land Mamma had prophesied.

Saint-Domingue looked smaller than Eni's home in Africa. Hundreds of palm trees dotted the island. Gone were the great dika trees of the kingdom land. As she de-boarded, the earth felt softer beneath her feet. Flying insects of every kind buzzed around her face.

"This is Port-au-Prince in Saint-Domingue," said a man in a whisper.

Eni tried to turn her head towards the voice, but her iron neck brace prevented it.

"I heard them talking on the ship," he said.

Eni finally recognized the voice as Mudia's. She recalled when they were on the ship, Mudia and other Africans worked very hard to decipher the French language. Remarkably, Mudia had learned much more than a few words.

"Where are we going?" she asked.

"To Claude Douleur's land in the northern plains. Claude is the fat White man. He bought us to work the land."

Eni felt the gentle rise and fall of Nya's body as she cuddled in her arms. To her astonishment, Nya was sleeping.

"Eni, we must stay together," said Mudia. "We must stay with our kinsmen. It is the only way we will survive."

Thierry snapped a whip at Mudia.

"Quiet!" he said.

Ships of all size littered the island's coast. Once off the port, the Africans were dragged naked through the middle of a bustling outdoor market. They moved sorrowfully through small vendor tents selling fruit, meat, vegetables, spices, and people. White women, fully dressed in elaborate gowns, accompanied by their children, were talking and laughing amongst themselves. Vendors called out their wares repeatedly, drowning each other out in a maddening cacophony. Eni saw brown men and brown women beautifully dressed. They looked African to her, but their skin tone was too light for her to be certain.

"Stop!" said Thierry.

Some of the Africans stopped, while others bumped into each other. Eni fell forward, accidentally dropping Nya on the dusty ground.

"Here, let me help you," said a woman.

Eni strained to see the woman standing over her. She, too, looked African but was light brown in skin tone. Her hair flowed like black rivers. Her eyes resembled the bright brown elk Eni used to hunt when she was a girl. The woman held Nya carefully, waiting for Eni to stand up. Clutching the neck chain with one hand, Eni reached for Nya with the other. The woman gave the child back, then flipped her long black hair before walking away.

A Plan

Douleur Plantation
Saint-Domingue
1799

The late afternoon sun beat against Nya's neck. She paused and wiped her face with a small dirty cloth that she kept tucked in her waist. Although a teen, she could barely keep up with the daily quota of cutting thousands of sugar cane stalks with machetes. Using a stalk for support, Nya straightened, then inverted her back to alleviate its soreness. Omorédé saw her from afar and snapped his fingers at her.

"Keep moving," he said in a French creole.

"You are not over us, so go away!" said Nya.

She glared at him as did the others.

"Princess, I am in charge here, not you," said Omorédé.

He spoke from atop a wooden platform he had made by himself. Omorédé, weak and thin, stood as tall as he could, trying desperately to tower over the slaves toiling in the Caribbean sun. Everyone ignored him. One assaulted him and pushed him down.

"You are *not* king. If there is any royalty here, it is Nya," said the assaulter.

Omorédé spat on the ground.

"I am the king," he said. "I am the son of the king. The master put *me* in charge."

At that, all who could hear him, laughed, including Nya who laughed the loudest. Douleur's overseers were nowhere to be seen.

"Omo," said Nya. "The day you become king is the day the French set us free without a fight. If that happens, I will personally give you my crown. Even Mudia will kiss you and bow."

Peals of laughter spread among the slaves in the fields. It was a brief comedic respite in the midst of brutality. Although none respected Omorédé, he had proven to be viciously dangerous. When pushed too far, he was known to spread wild rumors intended to infuriate Claude who, in turn, would kill a slave or two for insubordination.

Omorédé stamped his feet in anger then stormed off, slapping stalks out of his way. He headed toward the crushers where strong slave men worked 12 hours a day, using their sheer strength to move large wooden wheels connected to crushing beds. They crushed thousands of bundles of sugar cane stalks per day resulting in tons of sugar cane juice sent to the boilers.

Omorédé barged in, pushed his way through and immediately searched for a stool to stand on.

"Mudia! You are moving too slow," he said.

Unlike Omorédé, Mudia had physically strengthened through the years. The back-breaking slave work built every muscle in his body, it seemed. Although Claude despised Mudia's rebelliousness, he often marveled at Mudia's physical strength, calling him his best slave hand over Omorédé.

"Mudia! I said you are moving too slow," said Omorédé.

Mudia stopped and looked up. Omorédé trembled.

"Omo," said Mudia. "Go away."

"I am in charge here," said Omorédé.

"You are a slave, Omo."

"So are you."

"I will never be a slave."

"Mudia, don't think I am ignorant of what you are planning to do."

Mudia moved closer to Omorédé who immediately jumped from the stool and backed away.

"What am I planning to do, Omo?"

"If you touch me, I will tell Douleur."

"Tell him what?"

"That you tried to kill me."

"Omo, I am worth ten of you. You mean *nothing* to Douleur."

"Mudia, you are a rebel. Douleur hates rebels."

"And I hate Douleur."

"The overseers will hear you. They will blame me for your insubordination."

"Insubordination to what? to whom?"

"Mudia, please. I-I know the plan between you and Nya and the others."

Mudia grabbed Omорédé's arm and squeezed it.

"Omo, I am free. It is *you* that is a slave."

****

At the late supper meal, Mudia, Eni and Nya sat outside around a small fire. Nya had made an herbal medicine for Eni and was helping her to drink it.

"Drink, mother," said Nya.

Eni smiled weakly and sipped the sour liquid.

"Thank you, princess," she said.

"Mother, you have to eat, too. You need to break your fever," said Nya.

She offered Eni her plate of boiled plantains and cassava bread. Eni shook her head.

"No, princess. You need your strength more than me. Eat," she said.

"But if you don't eat, you can't return to work. Then Douleur will-"

"Nya, let her be," said Mudia. "Douleur will not

touch her. Eni, you will live in freedom, too."

Eni looked away.

"Please, Mudia," she said. "Do not talk of this tonight."

Mudia quickly looked around before responding.

"Eni, we must fight. We have come too far. Look at Mackandal. He was a hero," he said.

"Mackandal was killed for trying to poison the White man," said Eni.

"But he started something. It was just the beginning," said Mudia.

"Beginning of what?" said Eni.

"Mother," said Nya. "France is changing. There is talk of liberty for all people, including slaves."

"If that is so, why I am still here?" said Eni.

"Because White men will never give something for free," said Mudia. "They know how to take but not how to give. We must *take* our freedom from them."

Eni shivered.

"Princess," she said. "Your mother, the Queen, prayed for you. She was tired of sending her sons to die in battle. War is not for you."

"Mother, I will be leaving the plantation with Mudia," said Nya. "I want you to come with me. We will live in the free village in the mountains. The people there do not work for anyone but themselves."

Eni closed her eyes and sighed.

"Mother? Did you hear me?" said Nya.

"Princess, war is *not* for you. I forbid you to fight. You must survive, not fight," she said.

"To fight is to survive," said Nya.

"I think it is a mistake," said Eni.

"Then what do we do?" said Mudia. "Die in the stalks? Die from starvation? Die at Douleur's hand? We have to try, Eni."

"Douleur will find us and kill us. No, I must stay alive and keep Nya alive. That is what *I* must do," said Eni.

Nya leaned over and kissed Eni on the cheek.

"Mother, I love you. You have been my protector from the moment I was born. You have been my only source of love and strength. But I am stronger now. I know what I am doing. Let me protect you now. Come with us, please," she said.

Just then, a heavy-set slave woman named Kessie walked towards to where they were sitting. She, too, was from the Fon people but had been brought to the Douleur Plantation many years before.

"Eni, my sister," said Kessie. "It is late. You should sleep now. Maybe tomorrow you can work."

As Kessie she sat down next to Eni, Mudia stood up and dusted his pants.

"Until tomorrow," he said to the women.

He winked at Nya then abruptly left to return to his cabin.

"What is it, Eni, Nya?" asked Kessie.

"Kessie, do you know of free Africans living in the mountains?" said Eni.

"Mother!" said Nya.

Kessie patted Nya's shoulder.

"It is alright, Nya. Yes, I know. Everyone knows. Even Douleur knows. There are villages there, but it is *very* dangerous. Sometimes the White men go there and kill them," she said.

"But that has not happened since Mackandal," said Nya.

"No, it has not," said Kessie.

"Nya, you are a princess, not a soldier," said Eni. "Your plan is too dangerous. You will die."

"Mother, I must fight. I *must*," said Nya.

Kessie turned and draped her heavy arm around Eni's shivering body.

"Eni, if you were not my sister," she said. "I would tell you to stay here so that you and Nya will survive...but that is not the truth."

"What do you mean?" said Eni.

"Nya will not survive this life and neither will you," said Kessie.

"I don't believe that. Since I came here, Nya and I have had much luck. We are still alive. We are surviving," said Eni.

Kessie lowered her voice to a whisper.

"My sister, Nya is right. You *must* flee," she said.

"What you are suggesting is too hard, Kessie," said

Eni. I am sick and Nya is barely a woman."

"Mother, I am strong," said Nya. "I can help you."

Kessie rubbed Eni's back.

"My sister, Douleur will work us until we die. He will beat us and starve us to death. The sweetness of the sugar cane comes from our pain. I would rather live in the mountains then live in slavery," she said.

"They why don't you go, too?" asked Eni.

"Because I am too old. I was brought here years before you came. I have lived most of my life as a slave in Saint-Domingue. But I believe in the day for freedom. I heard the French King is under siege. There is great turmoil in France. Change is coming, sister. I can see it from afar, just like back home when we could see a storm rising in the west before it comes to the village," said Kessie.

"Do you think this will really happen?" said Eni.

"It must happen. I believe it," said Kessie.

"Then I will stay here with you," said Eni.

"Mother, no. Listen to Kessie. You must go with me," said Nya.

Kessie smiled.

"Sister, everyone knows that Mudia is a troublemaker! I am surprised he has not yet escaped. Go with him. Go with Nya. Follow them to freedom. It is your only hope," she said.

Kessie hugged her, then caressed Nya's face before standing up.

"Get some sleep, sister," she said before leaving for her quarters.

After Kessie left, Eni and suddenly began to cry.

"Nya, there is so much you do not know. I was there on the day you were born, the day King Fon fought his last battle and was defeated, the day we were sold to the White man."

"Mother, you already told me the story."

"No, Nya. I only told you that Mamma saved your life. I never told you that *you* saved my life. You gave me motherhood again. You gave me a second chance at loving a child. You saved my life, princess."

Eni wiped her face. She glanced at the night sky, trying to decipher the outline of the northern mountains.

Only dark shadows of their broad, rugged shoulders were visible.

Eni looked at Nya again.

"For you, princess…," she said in a whisper. "Just for you, I will go."

Plaçage

Jerémie, Saint-Domingue
1799

"Payment is late again!" said Claude.

"Darling, calm down. France will pay, they always do," said Madame Narcisse Douleur.

"No. It is different this time. There is no food, no money. People are angry. Twice those vagrants broke into our home in Paris. This revolution must end!" said Claude.

He banged his fist on the kitchen table with such force that it caused Narcisse to jump. She had not seen this side of her husband before. He was usually cool tempered, yet lately Narcisse had noticed the souring of Claude's mood as the turmoil in France intensified.

"If we cannot sell, we do not eat. Do you not understand this?" he said.

Narcisse did not respond but stood up to leave.

"Where are you going?" said Claude.

"To bed. It is late and I am tired," said Narcisse.

"Hm. Tired from what? Shopping in Port-au-Prince? Gossiping with your spoiled friends?" said Claude.

Narcisse quietly ascended the stairs without looking back. Once she was gone, Claude grabbed his hat and cane. He whistled to a slave and ordered him to prepare his riding gear. In minutes, Claude mounted his horse and left.

He galloped south on the dirt roads in the darkening night, stopping only to give his horse a break. He passed through Gonaïves, then Saint-Marc, then into Port-au-Prince. After taking a supper break at a saloon in the Port-au-Prince market square, Claude headed east, then south past Leogane, and the small city of Prestel. The island was filled with farmland of every abundant harvest. Claude could smell the pungent scent of cocoa beans, fragrant spices, peanuts and rum as he traveled. The scents reminded him of the pinnacle of success his sugar business had once enjoyed.

Claude continued west towards Jerémie, mulatto territory. Although long, Claude had taken this route so often, he had memorized every turn, every hill and every tree marking the way. Even in the twilight, Claude easily found his way to Fortunée's house. He tied his horse in her stable and rapped twice at the door. In seconds, it opened to a cream-colored woman with black wavy hair cascading down her back. She smiled sweetly and immediately ushered Claude inside.

"I thought you were coming tomorrow?" asked Fortunée.

Claude wrapped his arms around Fortunée and kissed her cheek.

"Am I not welcome?" he said.

"Oh, you are always welcome," said Fortunée.

The two walked towards the sitting room and sat on the couch. Claude ran his fingers through Fortunée's hair.

"Tell me, what have you been doing lately?" he asked.

"Oh, a little of this and a little of that," she said.

"Well, is it enough that you can spare me a loan?"

Fortunée laughed.

"A loan, from *me*? Are you trying to back out of our contract? I thought a deal was a deal."

"Oh, no. A deal is a deal. But I need a loan, just a little one. France is late with payment of my last shipment of sugar."

"And why is that my problem? Why don't you leave for New Orleans like all the others?"

Just then, a little girl, no older than two years old, wandered into the room. Her sleepy eyes opened wide when she saw Claude. She ran into his waiting arms.

"Papa!" she said.

"Ah, my darling. Why are you not in bed? It is late, no?" said Claude.

The little girl buried her face in Claude's arms. She giggled as he tickled her.

"Oh, enough, eh? Eveline, go to bed. Go!" said Fortunée.

Eveline slid down his leg and skipped past her mother. She gave Claude one last smile before disappearing out of the sitting room.

Fortunée turned to Claude.

"Now," she said. "What is this loan for? Do I add it to the contract? How will you pay me back?"

"We don't need to add it to the contract. I will deed you another part of my land as collateral."

"How can I be sure you did not deed it to your wife?"

"Because I did not. I will have the papers brought to you next week. You can see for yourself."

"Hm. I will think about it."

Fortunée stood up and walked into the kitchen. She returned with a flask of local rum and two drinking glasses.

"The finest for the finest."

She poured the rum into a glass and handed it to Claude. He drank it quickly.

"Fortunée, how long will you take to decide? If the people in France continue this revolt, that fat Louis will never pay me! I will have to sell to England and they will not pay my price."

Fortunée reclined next to Claude.

"My love, King Louis is not in control anymore. The rebellious Directory is gaining legitimacy among the Parisians."

"The Directory are not Frenchmen; they are pitiful peasants!"

"Either way, my love, they seem to be effective. Why, just last week I was reading in La Gazette Francoise that the Constituent Assembly will issue a 'Declaration of the Rights of Man and of the Citizen.' I read that *all* persons will soon be free and full French citizens."

"That may be so, but a document has nothing to do with reality. They will never make them free."

"*Them?*"

"Oh, you know what I mean. I speak of the slaves. The *black* African slaves."

"Do not forget, my love, I am the daughter of those whom you speak of."

"Yes, but you are privileged. Look at you. You are a sight of fair beauty. You are a perfect French woman."

"A perfect French woman with imperfect French

citizenship, no?"

"Do not worry. You have good wealth and status here. You do not need to be a full French citizen."

"Why not, my love? Do you wish for me to remain in the shadows?"

Claude looked at Fortunée.

"Why waste time over politics?"

"My love, it is not politics, but my life. You have a sprawling land full of free laborers who have made you wealthy. I have a house, a child, and a contract instead of a husband."

"Is that the problem? You want to marry?"

"It does not matter. It can never happen."

"I will not have some slave take my property, Fortunée! That was the arrangement. A deal is a deal, after all."

Fortunée shifted uncomfortably in her chair.

"How much do you need?"

"Two thousand."

Fortunée sipped her rum before responding.

"Give me your land."

Claude gulped.

"My land?"

"All of it."

"My land is worth much more than two thousand francs!"

"This is true my love, but it is true only now. France is at war. They will default. They cannot even pay the debts they owe to Britain. You will not be able to continue your business so profitably, causing your land in Saint-Domingue to be rendered worthless. So, you see, I am doing you a favor."

"As long as I have the labor, I will always have a profitable business."

"Oh, my love. You know the stories. The slaves are getting restless. Free labor may soon be difficult to find."

Claude chuckled.

"You are a shrewd businesswoman, Fortunée."

"I learned from the best, my love. Now, what do you say?"

Claude finished his rum and set it on the small table. He smoothed his hair and wiped the sides of his mouth.

"Do I have a choice?"

She laughed.

"I do not think so, my love."

"Well, then it is settled. I will have the deed sent to you next week."

Fortunée smiled and nodded in agreement. Then Claude took the glass from her hands and set it on the table. He stood up, took her hand and guided her to her bedroom upstairs.

"Now, Fortunée, let's finish with this talk of money. It is time to discuss other matters."

The Escape

The Northern Mountains,
Saint-Domingue
1800

"My sister, my daughter, hurry. If you do not leave now, you will never make it," said Kessie.

Nya wrapped Mamma's colorful scarf around her head. The she opened a cloth bag and filled it with bananas, mangoes, papaya and coffee beans. Eni stood next to her, shivering.

Kessie handed Eni a small medicine bottle.

"My sister, don't forget to drink it to control your fever," she said.

Then Kessie gave Nya an unlit kerosene lamp full of oil.

"Be careful with this, my daughter," she said.

Nya nodded, took the lamp and set it on the dirt ground. Then the women held hands while Kessie whispered a short prayer.

"The god of our ancestors," she said. "Please spare my sister and my daughter tonight. Bring them to freedom. Help them to liberate our people and bring justice to our land."

There was no more time to waste. Nya picked up the bag and slung it across her body while Eni held the kerosene lamp at her side. They kissed Kessie and fled, moving quickly and carefully out of the slave quarters. It was twilight on the Douleur plantation. A few slave women were busy at work behind the main house, preparing the Sunday breakfast for Monsieur and Madame Douleur. Eni and Nya stopped and waited for them to momentarily leave their work. Once it was clear, they continued through the fields towards the dense forest which outlined the plantation.

Eni and Nya walked slowly, deliberately crouching low so as to appear invisible within the tall sugar cane stalks. In what seemed like hours, they finally reached the edge of the forest. Its thick trees created a canopy of deep, terrifying darkness. Eni held the kerosene lamp up and lit it. It emitted a soft spotlight enabling them to see several feet ahead. Nya grabbed her hand and together they marched forward. Mudia had told Nya to move north through the forest until she reached a massive avocado tree. He said he would be waiting there to escort them onward to the mountain base. His only warning was to listen for unusual sounds and to step carefully for poisonous snakes and large lizards were abundant.

Eni and Nya moved tree by tree. They waited at each tree for a few seconds before moving to the next one. Nya listened for footprints or unusual rustling of trees, but all she could hear was the wild beating of her own heartbeat. She saw Eni sweating profusely as her body slightly shivered with each step.

Unbeknownst to the women, they were being followed. Many steps behind them was Omoréde, quietly tracking them like a bounty hunter. He had been listening at the slave quarters and stealthily remained on the women's path, moving from tree to tree.

"Where are you going?" said a voice.

The women froze.

"Who are you?" said the voice.

They heard branches crunching underfoot the anonymous person. Gradually, a young man emerged between the trees.

"What are you doing?" he asked.

The young man appeared to be Nya's age. He was not a French White boy nor an African boy. His skin color resembled the hue of tan leather. His straight shiny black hair was bound by a single long braid down his back. He was poorly dressed yet looked healthy and strong. He peered at Nya with curiosity.

"Where are you going?" he asked again.

"We are delivering a package to the Nicolas plantation in the north," lied Nya.

"You are slaves?" he said.

Suddenly, they heard a loud thud nearby. It was Omórédé who had tripped over an exposed tree root. He recovered quickly and crouched low so as not to be seen.

Nya responded to the young man in a whisper.

"We are from the Douleur plantation," she said.

His face suddenly brightened.

"What is the code word?" he said.

Nya looked at Eni who nodded as if to reassure her.

"Haiti," said Nya.

"Good. I will take you to Mudia," he said.

Despite the darkness, the young man skillfully hiked through the dense trees. The land gradually sloped upward, causing them to naturally slow in their pace. Omorédé kept behind him while successfully concealing his presence. They moved through the entire night. The tropical forest vibrated with buzzing insects, scurrying creatures, and melodious birds flying overhead.

Eni slapped at insects persistently poking her skin with their tiny stingers. As she raised her kerosene lamp around her, she exhaled in relief. Through its soft light, she could see a large avocado tree ahead. They continued climbing until they reached its great trunk. When Nya hugged Eni in quiet celebration, she noticed Eni's clothes were soaking wet so she leaned her mother against the tree to rest.

The young man stood at the base of the tree and made a bird call with his mouth. Seconds later, the top branches of the avocado tree suddenly swished and swayed. Small branches and stray leaves flew overhead as someone swiftly shuffled down the trunk. It was Mudia. Once on the ground, he smiled broadly at Nya and hugged her. Then he wrapped his arms around Eni's weakened body and slung her over his shoulder. Mudia turned to the young man.

"Bojé, let's go," he said. "Someone was following you."

****

"She suffered cruelty in Africa. She was captured and tormented on the high seas. She was expected to die - but she escaped death. She bore the pains of slavery with courage and strength. She was expected to die - but she escaped death. She shielded her girl-child with all her love, all her strength, all her mind. She was expected to die - but she escaped death. Then she bravely heeded the calls of liberty. In the name of Haiti, in the name of her beloved girl-child, in the name of the Fon people, she escaped slavery. She escaped slavery's humiliation. She escaped slavery's constant shadow of misery. And now she is free! She died in freedom. Now, she is free! May the gods of our ancestors bless Enibokun abundantly! May her ancestors guide her to her final home!"

As the old man spoke, he slowly sprinkled dust over Eni's burial mound.

"And may our Lord, Jesus Christ, bless Enibokun with the rewards of heaven," he said, making a sign of the cross in the air.

Battle Cry

A secret cave in the Northern Mountains
Saint-Domingue
1800

"We cannot wait any longer. The time is ripe. France is revolting!" said Nya.

She walked about confidently while speaking. Mamma's colorful headscarf was wrapped around her head.

"Nya, you want to move too fast," said Fortunée. "King Louis has lost power, this is true. But soon the Declaration will be in full force on the island. There is talk of a rebel raiser, Napoleon, that may seize the crown. Revolution is coming, brothers. We must wait."

She sat in the corner of a small cave filled with former slaves. The kerosene lamp next to her reflected the smoothness of her cream-colored skin.

Mudia sucked his teeth.

"How do you know, Fortunée? How can we trust

you? You are a White woman!" he said.

He had objected to Fortunée's presence but was overruled by a free African General named Toussaint L'Overture who, through his soldiers, ordered Nya to convene this meeting.

Omorédé was standing just feet away from Fortunée.

"Do not talk to her like that! She deserves your respect, Mudia," said Omo.

"Eh, the coward still thinks he can tell me what to do? I do not understand why a slave is here. You should have stayed in your chains where you were happy," said Mudia.

"You are acting like the animal that you are. Fortunée is a beautiful woman who deserves your respect. We should do as she says."

"The king's son is a coward. He can only do what the White people say, eh?"

Murmuring suddenly erupted among the group.

"Mudia, I have had enough of you."

"*You* followed me here, Omo. You are a threat and

cannot be trusted. Go back to Douleur."

"If it wasn't for me, Douleur would be here right now. I came to protect you and your princess. *I* am the one keeping Douleur away."

"Oh, is that so? How are you doing that? Through your White business with your White woman?"

"Do not speak of Fortunée that way. It is not your business."

"When your White business threatens my liberty, it *is* my business."

"Brothers," said Nya. "We cannot fight each other now. We are in the midst of turmoil. We must act with unity and peace."

Nya held her head high with her hands clasped behind her back. She strolled as she spoke. A sword slung across her body.

"Brothers," she said. "Saint-Domingue is at the brink of collapse. The weight of the cruelty and the tragic circumstance of slavery is causing its downfall. France's power is waning. They are not focused on Saint-Domingue because of the French civil war. They are too busy fighting each other like spoiled children!

Brothers, sister, listen! This is what Toussaint proposes. We take France into Spanish territory and conquer it for France. We will liberate our brothers and sisters there. Then, we will turn on France and claim Haiti as our own!"

"Impossible!" some of the men shouted.

"This cannot be done!"

"France will learn of it!"

Fortunée stood up to speak.

"Nya, as you know, I will support Toussaint's greater cause, but I still think we should wait. After all, what is the rush? France is burning as we speak. We should first let France fall," she said.

Mudia scoffed.

"This is a White woman! She is speaking this way because she will betray us!" he said.

Omorédé cleared his throat.

"Nya," he said. "I also do not agree with you. When France falls, they will free us. Then we will be French citizens. All this fighting is unnecessary. Besides, you are just a woman. You are not a soldier. In my father's kingdom, *I* was the prince. I have fought in invasions. I have been to battle. I have defended people and land by the sword. You have not."

"Omo, you were a coward then and you are a coward now!" said Mudia.

"Oh, Mudia, you are still hot-headed! In truth, you were the *worst* of my father's soldiers!" said Omorédé.

Mudia struck Omorédé on the side of his head. Omorédé stumbled briefly, then responded with a blow to Mudia's side. Soon, the two were tussling on the dirt floor while the assembly jeered.

"Brothers, brothers, stop!" said Nya.

Some men pulled them apart. Mudia wrestled out of their grips, then spat on the ground before storming out of the cave. Nya glared at Omorédé who was breathing heavily while leaning against Fortunée.

"We cannot have disunity now, brothers," she said. "We must let old disagreements die."

Some of the men applauded her words. One man spoke.

"Nya, I support the liberation," he said. "But France cannot be trusted. Do you not remember Mackandal?"

"My brothers, I hear your words," said Nya. "Mackandal lit the fire for us. He fanned the flames of freedom with his own blood. If that is the cost, then Toussaint says we must pay it."

"But I think you are mistaken. France will betray Toussaint," said the man again.

"Oh, do not worry about this," said Fortunée. "France does not have enough eyes in Saint-Domingue. Besides, Monsieur Sonthonax, that weak French negotiator, is on our side. My friends will supply you with everything."

Another man spoke up.

"Then what happens?' he said. "Fortunée, you are a mulatto. You are a landowner. Your people will try to enslave us again."

"Our interests are very much aligned," said Fortunée. "Whether we are free by the sword or decree, you and your people will get freedom from slavery. Me and my people, we will get our dignity. No longer will we be second-class French citizens who are treated as donkeys, scapegoats, and whores for the disgusting French White man."

"Then it is settled? We will move now?" said Nya.

Some of the men applauded in agreement while others remained silent.

"Princess, I am with you," said the man who had earlier protested.

At that, all laughed and cheered. They sang and chanted songs of freedom and military valor. Some broke out in traditional African dance. Omoréde was the only one who remained silent. He went to Nya and whispered in her ear.

"Nya, you are just a little woman," he said. "You are *not* a soldier. You do not have the authority to command an army. If there is anyone who should be in charge, it is me. *I* am royalty. I am the king. And there will *never* be a Haiti."

Nya smiled.

"Omo, I may just be a little woman," she said. "And I may just be a princess. In fact, I think I am the last princess of Saint-Domingue. But one glorious day, after our military victory, you and I will be among the first children of Haiti."

The End of the Douleur Plantation

Northern Plains
Saint-Domingue
1801

The Douleur plantation had burned overnight. It was rumored someone had deliberately set a fire in the sugar cane fields. Although the fire was eventually put out, miles of crops had already burned, destroying Claude's profits for months to come.

He was sitting in the living room, mulling over the events of the night before. He was alone, having sent his wife to New Orleans months ago.

"Bernard!" said Claude.

A slave man appeared almost instantly.

"Find out the status of the fields!" he said.

The slave nodded and disappeared. Claude shook his head. He was angry, exhausted, and incensed with France. In his mind, the French Consulate had forgotten its citizens abroad, leaving them to fend for themselves during the current slave revolts spreading throughout Saint-Domingue.

A sudden knock on the front door startled him. Having sent his house slave to run an errand, Claude had no choice but to open the door himself. Monsieur Léger Félicité Sonthonax was standing on the porch. He took off his hat and smiled.

"Monsieur Douleur," he said.

Claude stood back allowing the French Civil Commissioner to come into the sitting room. Sonthonax stepped into the house cautiously.

"Where is your servant?" asked Sonthonax.

"Why don't *you* tell me?" said Claude.

Sonthonax snickered.

"It is just like you to blame me. I am trying to keep some order here," he said.

Claude sat in a chair as Sonthonax sat opposite him. They stared at each other until Sonthonax spoke again.

"You know, Claude, things will have to change. It is the only way. I will *have* to free them," he said.

"And what about us? What about the real French

citizens who have been making France rich! What about us?" said Claude.

"You will all be compensated for your loss through the Indemnity. Besides, you may still be able to keep your land. I have a plan. They will work their own land for food only so as not to compete with trade. They will be forbidden to sell sugar, coffee beans, rice, or rum. They will also work the plantations for compensation, so the economy can continue."

"Why should I have to pay them? I already paid for my labor. I have to pay again? They burned my land! They destroyed my crops! This is nonsense!"

"Revolution is here. We must move forward."

"What do you know? You come here and think you understand Saint-Domingue? The King sends you here to create peace? You understand nothing!"

"That is where you are wrong. I was appointed Civil Commissioner of this part of Saint-Domingue for a reason. I am here to bring order and to continue profits. My colleague, Monsieur Polverel, is planning far more than me. He plans to allow them to *vote* and even hold office!"

"The only order is to return to the way it was."

"Monsieur Douleur, because of your people's torture and maiming and unnecessary killing of these slaves, they have revolted…and rightly so. No man can withstand such cruelty for long."

"'Your people'? You talk as if you are one of them? What deals have you made with them?"

"I am a Frenchman who is ready to swim with the coming tide. Those who do not move, will drown."

"If I drown, I am taking you with me."

Sonthonax stood up and placed his hat on his head.

"Claude…I take your leave."

Nya's Capture

Saint-Marc
Saint-Domingue
1801

"Oh, Omo, my love, do not worry," said Fortunée.

They were sitting at a small table in the back courtyard of Fortunée's house which overlooked the sea. Silver blue waves of the Atlantic Ocean sparkled beneath the morning sun.

"Omo, speak to me, please," said Fortunée.

Omorédé looked at her.

"Fortunée, you don't understand," he said. "I was a prince. I was the son of a king. How can Nya lead an army? Mudia is behind all of this. The whole thing is stupid."

Fortunée slumped in her chair, shivering slightly in her silk robe.

"What is wrong?" asked Omorédé.

"I feel as if you do not love me anymore," she said.

"That is not true."

"Then why won't you trust me?"

"Nya had us set the plantations on fire, burn the stores, burn the stalls, set the animals free, burn the crops. Look at Douleur. It is gone. There are just a few slaves left. He was supposed to leave, but he is still there. That is because Nya does not know what she is doing."

"Do not worry. Nya will be gone soon…and Claude is leaving. If he doesn't, I will urge him to leave."

"How do you know all this?"

"I have friends, Omo. Sonthonax is persuading all the landowners to take the Indemnity and abandon the land. It is just a matter of time before everything falls into place."

"We should have just waited for France. There will never be a Haiti. Slaves cannot run a country."

Fortuneé sat up and reached for Omorédé's hand. She placed her hand over his.

"Soon, we will be able to marry," she said.

"Fortunée, this is all that I want."

The couple momentarily gazed into each other's

eyes.

"And Omo, I think when this is all over, when Douleur is ours, maybe we can start a business."

"What kind of business?"

"Well, we can make sugar again. We will have to pay the laborers, but we will still be rich. You can be the director."

"Of course, Fortunée. I will do whatever you want. But this ridiculous chaos must work."

"Douleur will go. He will not fight me. He thinks I am the mother of his child."

Omorédé sucked his teeth.

"When are you going to tell her, Fortunée?"

"When she is older. She came out so light when she was born. It will be hard for her to believe that you are her father."

Omorédé looked away.

"Who is that?" said Fortunée.

Bojé appeared outside her courtyard gate. He was motioning for Omorédé to come out. When Omorédé saw him, he stood up and kissed Fortunée before leaving.

"What is it, Bojé?" asked Omorédé.

"There is a new development. You must return to the north immediately," said Bojé.

"What is the new development?"

"You will learn of it when you return. I have been told not to speak of it."

"I will return tomorrow morning."

"I have also been instructed to tell you to refrain from disclosing your departure to Fortunée."

"Fortunée? Why? She has supported our cause."

"It is best you tell her nothing. You will just have to leave before she can ask."

"Who gave you this order?" asked Omorédé.

"Mudia."

"Why not that little princess? Has she already been dethroned?"

"I wasn't supposed to say this here, but Nya has been captured. She was leading a band of soldiers to take the eastern plantations. The landowners revolted. She was captured along with other soldiers."

Omorédé could not help but to smile.

"Good. This is why she should never have been trusted to lead."

"Omo, you must return. The French army will be here any day. We need to save Nya. We need to save Haiti."

"I do not care about the princess. I will never fight for her. It is unnecessary. In fact, I am glad she is out of the way. I just want this chaos to be over so I can live in peace."

"But-"

"Tell Mudia to find another soldier. I do not care about his Nya and I do not care about his Haiti."

Fortunée's Sacrifice

Douleur Plantation,
Saint-Domingue
1801

Fortunée was careful as she stepped off her carriage. The land at Douleur was grossly neglected. Rocks littered the pathways. The once-green fields were scorched black, filled with charred sugar cane stalks. The plantation resembled that of an abandoned land in a war torn country.

She went to the front entrance. Then she breathed deeply before softly knocking on the front door. After several minutes, Claude opened it. He was disheveled. He had lost weight. Permanent lines were buried in his face. His eyes remained flat as he looked at Fortunée.

"What is it?" he said.

"Is that how you greet your love?" said Fortunée.

Claude left the door open and returned to the kitchen. Fortunée cautiously stepped inside. Clothes were strewn about. Dirty cups and plates sat on every open space. A sour smell graced her nose as she moved towards the kitchen.

"Claude, I have not seen you in some time. I miss your wonderful presence."

"What do you want?"

"I have come to talk terms, my love."

"What terms?"

"Well, I have learned you are preparing to board for New Orleans in the coming days. However, you have not repaid the loan."

Claude sipped black coffee from a dirty cup.

"Claude, my love?"

"I owe you nothing."

Fortunée cleared her throat.

"Must we settle this before the lawyers?"

"I told you, I owe you nothing."

"My love, must I return to Sonthonax's people and inform them of the change in ownership?"

"You cannot do that."

"And why is that, my love?"

"Because you do not own this land. *I* do."

"My love, you defaulted on the loan. The deed has been passed to me. See?"

Fortunée reached into her bag and drew out a piece of paper. She unfolded it and laid it before Claude to see.

"You see, my love. The lawyer has already prepared the deed. It just needs your signature."

"I left France and came to this wretched island with plenty of money. Now I must leave penniless because the Crown cannot control them?"

"My love, you know I am not one for politics. All I know is that a deal is a deal."

"I will never leave."

"My love, do not make this difficult."

"I will *never* leave."

"But how will you make money, my love. Your land is gone. The slaves are revolting everywhere. The ships are leaving."

"You think you are sophisticated with your papers? You think I am this dumb! You do not know me, Fortunée!"

He stood up and grabbed her arm.

"I know all about your excursions, you half-breed! I know all about that runaway slave you have been sleeping with. Yes, I have people, too."

Fortunée smiled tepidly.

"My love, those are all rumors. How could a woman resist a man like you?"

"Don't patronize me! *I* built this business. You did not. In fact, my uncle worked your slave mother to death. You are nothing but a slave's child!"

He squeezed her arm causing her to wince.

"I am one step ahead of you, Fortunée."

"What are you saying, my love?"

"Your mother was a slave. My uncle owned her. He once owned this land. Now, I own this land. So *you* belong to *me*. And you have been colluding with rebel savages. The penalty for such treason is death."

"My love, you must be mistaken. I am a free woman with French papers. I own property. What business do I have with slaves?"

Claude drew her close. He whispered into her ear.

"I know your daughter is his."

Fortunée swallowed.

"What, my love?"

"You heard me. I have people, too, Fortunée. I have proof. I have witnesses. That's why I kept that filth close to me. I had him watched and he led me right to you."

"My love, this cannot be. I would never betray you."

Claude slapped Fortunée so hard she spun around and fell to the floor. She laid there, groaning and rubbing her face.

"Fortunée, I am having you bound and hanged for insubordination. Tell that to that French traitor, Sonthonax."

"My love, perhaps we can discuss this. Perhaps we can settle this matter in a civil manner."

Claude sat down and smiled at her.

"You are nothing but trash, Fortunée."

"My love, please. There has to be some way to resolve this discrepancy."

"You want to resolve this? Stop your little rebellion and I won't have you killed."

"My love, there is no rebellion. There is no-"

"Fortunée, do not lie to me. I have your little savage leader hanging right now. I should have killed that little girl and her mother years ago. They cost me more than they were worth."

"Nya?"

"Is that what you people call her? She refused to speak to me. It does not matter. She is dying."

"My love, I have only heard of this rebel leader. I do not know her."

"Good. Once she is dead, I will have her body hung in Port-au-Prince so all can see. I have my men looking for your filthy paramour right now. He will hang alongside her. Your little slave daughter will hang beside him. And I will keep going until all those savages are hanged."

Fortunée swallowed.

"Is such violence necessary, my love?"

"So, you *do* love him."

"My love, it is you I desire."

"Fortunée, I will give you the savages for the land. Take them and leave. Never set foot here again."

"My love, that is not a fair trade. We had a deal. Besides, I have no use for a rebel leader."

Claude stood up and towered over her. She flinched, then gingerly pushed herself off the floor and stood up. Fortunée patted her perfectly pinned hair and breathed deeply.

"My love, you may discard of the deed as you wish. It seems my destiny no longer intersects with yours. Tell me where Nya is and I will say my farewell."

Claude threw back his head and laughed giddily.

"You lost! Without all your adornments, you are just like them. You are a slave, just like them."

"My love, where is Nya?"

"In the shack behind the boilers."

Fortunée turned and strode calmly out of the house. Once outside and out of Claude's view, she picked up the sides of her skirt and ran across the open field towards the boilers.

A Tip

A secret cave in the Northern Mountains
Saint-Domingue
1803

Nya was seated on a chair facing a small group of soldiers. She had finished discussing strategy and was now encouraging them before an expected battle with the French army.

"Brothers," said Nya. "Do no fear. We can win this battle. Toussaint L'Ouverture has guaranteed it."

"But, Nya," said a soldier. "We are out-numbered. We do not have enough equipment or supplies."

Mudia, who had been sitting next to her, stood up angrily.

"That is because that White woman betrayed us," he said.

"Mudia, she saved me," said Nya.

"No, she saved herself. She does not care about us

or Haiti. She just cares about herself," he said.

"What does it matter?" said the soldier. "We are still ill-equipped to fight."

"We have advanced successfully. We have already taken part of Saint-Domingue," said Mudia. "We can still defeat them."

"Mudia, I am not ready to die," said a soldier. "I have a family. I want to live."

"Brothers," said Nya. "We cannot be afraid of life or death. Years ago, when I has hanging, waiting to die, I saw my past, my present and my future. I saw my mother, the Queen, beautiful and regal, caressing my face and holding me tenderly. Her eyes dripped with love for me. I saw in her eyes my past. I heard her prayers for me. I felt her joy when she gazed upon my face at my birth. Then I saw an old woman, a prophet from my kingdom. She told me my future, that a life of freedom awaited. In fact, this life is at the door knocking. It is a life free from slavery and wretchedness. This woman strengthened my hope. She spoke of such freedom as if it was certain and true. And when I was rescued by Fortunée, I saw my present.

We are few, but when joined with L'Ouverture's men, we are many. We *have* defeated the French and we will defeat them again. If we do not fight, we will not be able to live."

"Nya, you speak well," said Fortunée.

She strode into the cave with her head held high. Mudia blocked her way.

"What are you doing here?" he said.

"Mudia, I came to pledge my support," said Fortunée.

"What support? You almost left her to die," said Mudia.

"Years ago, I made a deal with the devil," said Fortunée. "So I was not as charitable as I should have been towards Nya."

"Fortunée," said Nya. "I do not hold anything against you. Please join us."

"Nya, she cannot be trusted," said Mudia.

"Princess, I have information that may be of interest to you," said Fortunée.

She gently pushed past Mudia.

"What is it?" asked Nya.

"There is a man by the name of General Rochambeau of the French military. He has mobilized at the Artibonite River," she said.

"We already know this," said Mudia. "They will be advancing in two days at the port at Pierrot."

"This is not true. My men tell me they will be advancing at day break tomorrow," said Fortunée.

"Are you sure?" asked Nya.

"My men have heard General Rochambeau speak of it," said Fortunée.

Nya looked around.

"Where is Bojé?" she said.

"You mean, your love?" said a soldier.

Several soldiers laughed.

"Bojé!" said Nya.

No one answered from among the group.

"I will get him," said Mudia.

After he left, Fortunée turned to her.

"Princess, it has been some time since we have met. The whole affair with Douleur was most unfortunate," she said.

"We are on the cusp of victory, Fortunée. All that matters is that we are free."

"Princess, I have always believed in Haiti."

"Have you, Fortunée?"

"Of course, Princess."

"Where is Omo?"

"He is in New Orleans with our daughter. I sold my property so I am staying here with a friend."

"You stayed behind to give me this tip?"

"No, Princess, I stayed behind to support you."

"I see."

"And Princess, when we finally gain independence, my support would deserve just a small payment. Perhaps some land would be fitting? Perhaps you can speak to Toussaint about it?"

Nya looked at Fortunée. She was about to respond when Bojé ran into the cave and knelt before her.

"What is it, Nya?" he said. "Mudia said you called for me."

"Can you take a few men and reconnoiter the French military along the Artibonite River?" said Nya. "We have word they are mobilizing to advance at day break."

"Of course, Nya. Anything for you," said Bojé.

She smiled while he kissed her hand tenderly. Then he stood up and ordered a couple of soldiers to follow him out.

The Night Before

Cap-Français
Saint-Domingue
1803

It was the night before a battle at Vertières, a valley south of Cap-Français. The French army were camped just a few hundred feet away, separated from L'Ouverture's army by a winding trench. Nya had integrated her soldiers among a larger brigade in L'Ouverture's army. They were outfitted and restless, sharpening their swords and filling their guns with powder. Some soldiers joined in tribal African dance while others sat quietly, contemplating death. A few soldiers, like Mudia, were encouraging each other, remarking of the previous battles fought and won against the French and their proxies.

Nya chose to steal away and look at the stars. Eni had often told her the spirits of the Queen and Mamma lived within the stars. So she sat on the ground. She took

Mamma's headscarf from her waist and tied it around her head.

"Mother, Queen, Mamma," she said while looking at the sky. "Will I live through this?"

"Nya, who are you talking to?"

It was Bojé. He emerged from the darkness and sat down next to her.

"I was talking to…my mothers."

"Your mothers?"

"Yes. My ancestors."

"Nya, this might be the one."

"The one what?"

"The final battle. Mudia said France is in trouble. Napoleon is bankrupt. They cannot hold Saint-Domingue anymore. We have cost them too much money and too many men."

"I hope he is right."

"Nya, when it is over, marry me."

Nya looked at Bojé.

"What?"

"I am fond of you."

"Bojé-"

"We will live together in Haiti. We will bring new life on new land."

Bojé took her hand and kissed it. Then he kissed her cheek.

"Bojé, we are on the eve of battle. Death is all around us."

"Then we must live for Haiti. We must live for us."

A soft warm wind suddenly shifted around them. It ruffled through Mamma's headscarf, causing it to unravel and flutter down, landing atop Nya's sword. She removed it, then slid her finger along the blade.

"Bojé, if we survive this…."

"Yes?"

Nya wrapped her hand around her sword's hilt.

"Then I will belong to Haiti…and to you."

****

The battle at Vertières was the final major battle before the African slaves won their independence from France.

Saint-Domingue became Haiti, the first free Black Republic in the new world.

COVER ART BY

DORA ALIS

www.dora-alis.com

Made in the USA
Las Vegas, NV
07 August 2021